Evie and the Volunteers

Animal Shelter

Book 1

By: Marcy Blesy

Cover design by Cormar Covers.

Follow my blog for information about upcoming books or short stories. www(dot)marcyblesy.com

Chapter 1:

It all started the summer before my fifth grade year. I blame my mom who decided to go back to work the day after I stepped out of Mrs. McClintock's fourth grade classroom, *the very next day.* She didn't even think about the fact that I'd like to spend a little summer vacation time with her before she started her new job. I mean, who would take me to the beach or the pool or shopping or to The Dairy Cow to get an ice cream sundae? How could she be so selfish?

Mom woke me up every morning at 8:00 a.m. on her way out the door to her job at the International Tutoring Center. She'd been taking online Spanish classes to brush up on her college degree (from like a hundred years ago) and decided she should use her education to help others to get better jobs. I guess she taught English to Spanish-speaking adults or something like that. I thought she should care more about what her ten-year-old daughter wanted. Instead, I'd have to get myself out of bed when she left, get dressed, and cross the street to Grandma and Grandpa's house by 8:30 a.m. for breakfast or Grandpa would be mad at me for making his eggs cold. Grandma wouldn't let him eat until I got there.

It's not that I didn't like my grandparents. They were cool enough for grandparenty stuff like buying you dessert when you went out to eat or cheering for you at the band concert, but they weren't exactly the people I'd have picked to spend my summer with. Mom wouldn't listen to anything I said about why she should let me stay home alone.

Me: *I'm responsible. I'm smart. Everyone else gets to have a fun summer but me.*

Mom: *Evie, you're only ten-years-old. Do you know that I could get in trouble with the police for leaving a ten-year-old home alone all day?*

I didn't believe her, though, because my best friend Logan stayed home alone for half the day every Saturday so her parents could go on a date, which always seemed a little strange to me, but I knew better than to argue with my mom. I never won an argument with her, *ever,* and the few times I pushed it, like when I wanted to go to the movies with Clark Rogers, she'd grounded me from the television for even thinking of the idea. She thought I was boy crazy, but that's not true at all. It's just that Clark Rogers promised to give me some super cool Pokemon card (that I can't even remember now) if I went to the movies with him. He's a nice kid, but I really wanted that Pokemon card. Plus, my best friend Logan was going to the movies, too. She's been my best friend since the day we were born.

Really. We were born two hours and twenty-three minutes apart at the same hospital. Our moms became instant friends bonding over all that stuff you don't know when you first become a mom. Even though Logan was going to the movies, I couldn't go because Clark would be there, too. I really wanted that Pokemon card. That's when I thought those cards were still cool.

During the day, Grandpa and I would work on a 1000 piece puzzle of some city skyline of Chicago or New York City. Grandpa still dreamed of moving back to Chicago where he'd grown up, but since Grandma was born and raised along the shores of Lake Michigan, *on the right side of the pond,* she'd say, there was little chance that Grandpa would ever get his way. So, I made him happy by building his puzzles even though it wasn't easy. Their black cat, Mr. Stinkypants, had a bad habit of stealing puzzle pieces. He only took the edge pieces which was really weird.

And while Grandpa and I fought Mr. Stinkypants for the puzzle pieces, Grandma saved the environment crocheting plastic beach bags. She saved all of the plastic bags from the grocery store, cut them into strips, tied the strips together into a big ball that looked like yarn, and crocheted away while she sat in her chair and watched old episodes of *Family Feud*. The fun nearly dripped from my skin. *Not*.

One day that summer, Logan came over for some of Grandpa's famous homemade butter pecan ice cream. We ate lunch and played with Mr. Stinkypants until we got so bored we thought our heads would fall off our bodies and float away into space. That's when Logan had the great idea to ride our bikes down to the beach. We wanted to see who the cool kids were that weren't babied by the adults in their family like we were. Since Logan's parents thought she was safe at my grandparent's house, I was the one that needed to sneak out. I waited until Grandma went to the store to buy more groceries that she really didn't need and Grandpa was comfy in his chair waiting for his afternoon nap which he always took during reruns of *The Simpsons*. I closed the back door quietly and followed Logan across the street to my house. I used the code on our garage door to get inside, hoping the whole time that Grandpa had already fallen asleep and wasn't watching out the front window that faced our house. My bike was in the back corner of the garage under an old tarp. It hadn't been touched since my dad left a few months ago. We'd ridden our bikes on the Kal-Haven Trail near Kalamazoo. Dad seemed like he could have ridden for days. I was so tired! He had only been back from the war this time for a few weeks. He just didn't act normal. Something was different after his last tour of duty overseas. So, he went away for a little bit of time. I don't know much more. No one tells me important stuff.

As I pulled my bike out of the garage, I accidentally knocked over my dad's old motorcycle which was also under the tarp. I didn't even realize he hadn't taken it with him when he left. He'd loved that motorcycle. I suppose I should have realized that knocking it to the ground would be a sign to my mom that I'd been at our house during the day. I thought I could make up some excuse like maybe there had been an invasion of giant rats in our garage. Anyway, the sun was up and blazing, and we needed to get to the beach during prime *seeing people* hours.

When Logan and I arrived at the beach, there was a lot going on. We didn't know which direction to go. There were so many people we knew, starting with Logan's older brother's friends, to some of our classmates whose parents either brought them to the beach or trusted them enough to go there alone, to strangers visiting from Illinois who were having all kinds of fun playing volleyball or tossing

Frisbees. We dumped our bikes at the bike rack and raced each other down the beach. The first person who called to us was Franny Perkins. She and her little sister were scooping sand for sand castles, not my first pick for beach fun, but it was a start. I hadn't built a sand castle for years and decided I could probably become an expert at age ten now that I knew what I was doing. When Franny's little sister started whining about being hungry, we ditched the sand castle, the waves washing away my masterpiece. Franny, Logan, and I joined an exciting Frisbee game with some classmates who were brave (or stupid) enough to be standing waist-deep in the still cold June waters of Lake Michigan. Several hours later, I'm not sure when exactly, Franny pointed up the beach to the parking lot. *I wonder what all those flashing lights mean*, she'd said. But it didn't take long to figure it out when I heard my name being broadcast from the bullhorn of a policeman who was standing on the boardwalk. *Evie Quin. Evie Quin, if you are here, please report to the boardwalk immediately.* And to think that I thought that having to spend the summer at my grandparent's house was bad enough. Little did I know that my free days were about to become very limited.

Chapter 2:

I'm living through week number two of *Destroy Evie Quin's Life*, at least that's what I'm calling it. I'm convinced that Mom rewards herself with a shopping trip or a lunch out or something every time she feels like she's given me a better punishment than the one before. She blamed me for *nearly giving Grandma a heart attack* (her words) because of my *irresponsible and crazy behavior*. Plus, Grandpa missed his afternoon nap when they sent out the armed guards to find me. Well, it seemed like the whole police force was there at the time. I was so embarrassed. Then Mom found out I'd knocked over Dad's motorcycle. I didn't think it was such a big deal since if it had really been that important to him, he would have taken it when he left, but Mom carried on and on about the big dent in the side and how mad Dad was going to be and how I was going to have to pay for it because Dad didn't have the money. *Why doesn't he get a job?* I wanted to ask. That time I stayed quiet.

Of course, Mom knows I don't have any money, either. I figured with time, the whole thing would be forgiven. However, then she realized that my bike had also been stolen the day I went to the beach. Yes, I carelessly forgot the bike lock after having it drilled into my head for years to take care of the things I own. Adding up the near grandparent heart attack plus Dad's dented motorcycle plus my missing bike, and the idea of simply grounding me for a couple weeks became like the wimpiest punishment ever. I knew something way worse was coming.

Chapter 3:

"Mom, I *know* I screwed up. I promise I won't sneak out again. You have to believe me!"

"Evie, you can't go through life thinking that saying *I'm sorry* is all you need to do to make up for your mistakes. At some point your words are just that…*words*. You need behavior that backs up what you say. Volunteering at the Betsy Willis Animal Shelter will provide the perfect chance for you to learn responsibilities and do some good," says Mom.

If I thought that stomping my foot in protest would have been effective, I'd do it right now, but something tells me that I'd only make things worse and help Mom prove her point. Maybe I am a little irresponsible. Maybe I am a little selfish. But isn't that how ten-year-old girls are supposed to be? "Mom, I won't know anyone at the shelter.

That's not fair." I'm really trying hard to resist the need I have to stomp my foot.

Mom ruffles the top of my hair like Dad used to do when I was a little girl. I bet if she'd let me dye my dark hair blue like I wanted to do the last time I was at the hairdresser, she wouldn't be treating me like I was a little girl now.

"Actually, you will."

I roll my eyes, expecting her to tell me that some old woman from church works at the front desk at the animal shelter or that my older sister's ex-boyfriend scoops poop out of the cages. "Sure, Mom," I say.

"Logan's parents have decided that Logan needs to accept some responsibility for being so careless, too." Suddenly my punishment is getting a lot better. "But you're there to work."

"Yes, and I will become more responsible and learn to appreciate my life," I say sarcastically, repeating the words that Mom has been pounding in my head since my *escape*. That's what she insists on calling my trip to the beach. "How much will I make?" I ask.

"Make?" Mom puts her hands on her hips and raises her eyebrows in a triangle above her eye. "Evie, you are putting in volunteer hours at the animal shelter. You're not *making* anything."

I can't believe what I am hearing. "But, Mom! You mean I have to scoop poop and spend hours with flea-covered animals for *free?*"

"I very much mean exactly that," she says. "Go change. I'm dropping you off in half an hour." She leaves the room before I can even get in another word, not like it would even matter. My summer is officially over. I've been sentenced to community service.

Chapter 4:

The Betsy Willis Animal Shelter was built three years ago to help with the overpopulation of dogs and cats in Barrien County. Mom gives me a quick history lesson in the car. Betsy Willis is some rich lady who never had any kids of her own but always had a litter of dogs or cats living with her until she got sent by her sister to live in a retirement home when she got too sick to live alone. It sounds to me like she was the typical crazy cat lady you hear about in the news. Mom said she had a lot of money from some patent she created for a slow-feeding pet food dispenser. Maybe she wasn't so crazy after all. Then she gave away almost all of her money to her nephew, and he started this animal shelter in her name. She had almost nothing left after that.

We drive up the winding lane to the Betsy Willis Animal Shelter. Newly planted trees line both sides of the paved driveway. The animal shelter sits at the top of the hill overlooking the countryside. If I have to spend my punishment working with animals, even though I've never owned a pet in my life, at least I'll have a pretty view to take in during my breaks.

"Behave yourself, Evie," Mom says as we walk toward the front door. "Logan's mom will bring you home in the afternoon. Remember to thank her."

"You want me to thank Logan's mom for co-planning for us to spend our summer with stinky animals?" I ask, rolling my eyes.

"Yes, I do," Mom says quietly.

I hate it when she gets quiet. "I will be good, Mom," I say. "*Evie and the Volunteers*, hooray!" I say, pumping my fist in the air. "You have to admit it has a catchy ring to it."

Mom smiles while shaking her head. Why couldn't I have gotten the perfect child genes like my older sister Meredith? Maybe if we were closer than ten years apart, some of her *good kid* genes would have rubbed off on me— although I know that Mom wishes Meredith called home more often.

The woman at the front desk is not someone from church after all. She's a large woman, more a young Mrs. Claus-type with an easy smile. I can imagine she has a plate of cookies behind the counter with frosting and sprinkles that she passes out just because she can.

"Good morning," she says. "I'm Janet. How can I help you?"

I stop myself from asking for a sugar cookie. Mom is looking at me with *the eye* that's famous for meaning *you'd better get this right*. I extend my hand across the desk. "Hi, Janet," I say. "I'm Evie Quin. I'm here for my prison term…" Mom not-so-politely clomps on my foot. "I mean, I'm here to volunteer." I point to my mom. "I think she called."

Janet smiles, I'm sure of it, though she hides it well behind a folder she is holding with her other hand. "Nice to have you here, Evie. Your friend Logan is already in the back with Dr. Mick. You can head through that door." She points to a white door behind her desk that is covered in stenciled paw prints. How charming. I don't even say *goodbye* to my mom.

Logan is in the back, as promised. She has a cute, new haircut. I wish I was that brave to cut my hair. Her strawberry blonde hair is bobbing at her shoulders and bouncing up and down as she laughs at whatever the guy that must be Dr. Mick is saying. Dr. Mick is wearing blue scrubs like they wear at hospitals. He has a ponytail and a scruffy five o'clock shadow. That's how my mom used to describe Dad's face on Sunday nights when he'd gone all weekend without shaving. I thought everyone grew facial hair that fast until I stayed at Logan's house for a summer when I was six-years-old. It took her dad a whole month to grow anything close to looking like a beard. Mom and Dad went on some humanitarian trip through our church that summer. I could not understand why they'd want to leave their kids home in America to go wandering through some jungle in South America living with only the bare minimum when they could have been home, safe in Michigan with me. I'm not even positive what they were doing.

"Evie!" Logan yells when she sees me. "Come here. You have *got* to see this kitten. Isn't it adorable?" She shoves a pumpkin-colored cat into my hands. I don't mean to throw it, well, toss it really, but when it starts screaming the minute it's in my hands and lays a track of scratch marks on my forearm, it's the only logical reaction. "Evie!" This time Logan isn't yelling with joy.

"I'm sorry!" I yell, as blood trickles down my arm. "The cat hurt me." I show my arms to Logan and Dr. Mick, hoping to get some sympathy. Logan ignores me and goes chasing after the kitten. It is hiding under a cage.

"Let's get that cleaned up," says Dr. Mick. "I should have warned you that Sammy was a new resident with a long set of nails." He chuckles to himself as he guides me to the sink where he washes my arm with soap and water. He puts on anti-bacterial ointment and a bandage. "You'll be fine. Maybe next time you should sit on the ground and let the kitten approach you," he says. "I'm Dr. Mick, by the way." He sticks out his hand. I shake it, but I don't have the voice to tell him that I won't be holding any more cats. If I did speak right now, I'd tell him how messed up it was that I was having to spend the next two weeks coming to this horrible place every day. "Girls, let me introduce you to some of our residents."

Logan puts Sammy back in his...*her?* cage and follows Dr. Mick and I through another door into a large room that gets louder and louder with barking. *Loud barking.*

"I've got to get back to the clinic," Dr. Mick says. "Denise will take care of you girls from here. Be careful."

"Why is he dressed like that?" I ask Denise, the older woman who is waiting to talk to us after Dr. Mick has walked back out the door. The dogs calm down after they figure out that no one else is coming into the room.

"He's a doctor," she says, looking at me like I am crazy. "He doesn't dress up for surgeries."

"You mean a veterinarian?" asks Logan.

"Yes. He does spay and neuter surgeries for us once a month and comes out to check on the patients the next day. That's why he was here today," she says.

"What are spay and neuter surgeries?" I ask.

Denise smiles. "Female patients are spayed and male patients are neutered so that they cannot have babies."

"That's so cruel!" I say. "The poor animals don't have any choice!"

Logan shakes her head at me like she can't understand what I just said. "Evie, places like the Betsy Willis Animal Shelter exist because there are more dogs and cats than homes to take them in. The doctor is trying to reduce the population so that hopefully some day *all* animals will have a home." I stare at my best friend. How does she know all this stuff? She seems to read my mind. "We had our old dog Gracie spayed so she wouldn't have puppies. Think about it."

"Come on, girls. These animals can't feed themselves." We follow Denise to the corner of the large room where there is some sort of work station. Containers of food hang from the wall with knobs to turn that give out equal portions of food into the metal bowls that sit in piles on the table. Denise hands us each a bowl. "Every dog needs a food bowl. Slide it under the gate of each cage. There's an opening. Don't go into a kennel, or cage, without permission from me. Not all of these animals are friendly."

"If they're anything like the kitten I met this morning, I understand!"

"A new kitten acts on instinct," Denise says. "Some of these dogs have been trained to fight."

"Trained to fight?" asks Logan.

"Why?" I ask.

25

"People will pay to see dogs fight. They bet on the fights like a boxing match. It's against the law." Denise leaves us to go do the rest of her paperwork, leaving Logan and I to fill the dog food bowls. I can't stop thinking about what she's said. No wonder no one wants these dogs. Are they going to live out their lives in this plain, boring place?

"Come on, Evie. We have to feed the dogs now," says Logan.

It's easy to find the dogs that Denise told us about. They are large, muscular, and loud. Don't they realize I'm here to help them? To feed them? I start sliding the food bowl along the concrete floor from outside the cage. That way I won't get my fingers bitten.

Thankfully, most of the dogs are happier. These dogs wag their tails when they see Logan and I arrive with bowls of food. I wonder if this is their favorite part of the day. Kind of sad if it is. The last dog in the row of kennels I am feeding is neither aggressive nor happy. She is little, a pretty brown and white color. Her tiny body does not match her large head. It looks like it belongs on the body of another dog. Her tail hangs between her legs, and she edges closer to the back corner of her kennel than even seems possible as she sees me.

I get down on my knees and place the bowl on the floor next to me. The tag on the front of the cage tells me the dog's name is Daisy. She lets out a soft yap as if to tell me to stay away, but not even a baby would be intimidated by that sound. I push the bowl slowly through the slit in the bars of the kennel. Most dogs drag the bowl closer to them before I've even gotten the bowl halfway through the opening. Not Daisy. "Come on, girl," I say. "Aren't you hungry, little miss?" She doesn't take her eyes off me. I see the latch on the kennel door and don't give myself a chance to think about what I am about to do. I unlatch the door, pick up Daisy's bowl, and enter the cage. An ear-piercing scream meets my ears, a sound so pathetic one would think whoever was causing another living being to make such a noise was only up to no good or causing terrible harm, neither of which would be true. But I don't have time to explain myself. Denise is at my side pulling on my arm to remove me from Daisy's cage before I even have a chance to say anything.

"What do you think you're doing?" Denise asks. Her eyes scream at me like she's shooting death rays in my direction.

"Yeah, Evie. What did you do to that dog?" asks Logan.

"I didn't *do* anything," I say. I can feel tears forming in my eyes. The last thing I want to do is show my real feelings. I use the back of my hand to bat at my eyes. "She wasn't eating. I was trying to *help*."

"Well, you sure did a great job of that, didn't you?" says Denise.

"What's going on, ladies?" asks Janet, the lady from the front desk with the big smile. I sure could use one of her imagined sugar cookies right now to make this better.

"She entered Daisy's cage," says Denise.

"Oh," says Janet. She nods her head as if there is some secret that everyone knows but me.

I wish someone would tell me what is going on here. Janet puts her hand on my arm, a lot more gently than Denise, and leads me away from the cage. As we walk away, I notice that Daisy has taken a few steps and is pulling the bowl toward her. I can't help but grin.

"Daisy is a special dog—well, they all are, of course—but Daisy's been through a bit more than our other guests," says Janet.

I think *guests* is an odd word choice since guests can come and go as they please. I sure don't see that happening here. "I was just trying to help," I say quietly.

"I know. And we should have taken more time to go over our rules." I don't mention that Denise already gave us the rules. "There is to be no entering the kennels unless a staff member gives those directions. Sometimes it's for our protection, and sometimes it's for the dog's protection, like in the case of Daisy."

"The dog's protection? I wasn't going to hurt the dog."

"Daisy has been with us for a month. We almost didn't accept her. She was in such bad shape that we didn't think she'd make it through the night, but Dr. Mick was here at the time checking on patients. He worked his magic and told us to give her some time. Of course we've all fallen in love with her now, but since she's been through…so much...well, she's not going to be easily adopted. This shelter does not keep animals forever. If we cannot find a home for them, then they must be sent to a larger shelter in a bigger town."

"What if Daisy still can't find a home there?"

"We want all of our animals to be placed in loving homes, not live in cages the rest of their lives," says Janet.

I nod my head like I understand, but I don't. What could have happened to this dog that would make it unadoptable? She sure looks cute enough to me. "Janet, if Daisy does not get adopted, will she live the rest of her life in a cage?" Janet looks away but not before I see the sad look on her face, and I know the answer.

Denise interrupts my conversation with Janet. "Come on, girls. We have more work to do." Denise points to yet another door that leads to more adventure or trouble. I'm not sure which. Logan and I follow her to the door, but one more peek at Daisy puts an even bigger smile on my face when I see that her food bowl is empty.

Chapter 5:

I have a turkey sandwich waiting for Mom on a plate at the kitchen table next to a large glass of iced tea when she gets home. Grandma let me go home by myself after *Wheel of Fortune* since Mom had called and said she was leaving the tutoring center soon. After Logan's mom dropped me off at my grandparent's house, I spent the afternoon learning how to crochet with Grandma's plastic bags. I could not explain my sudden interest in learning Grandma's hobby. I'd always thought it was such a weird idea. I just have a need to spend some good time with her today. Every living animal should feel loved, whether it's a Grandma or a dog or a cat.

"Evie, what's the matter?" asks Mom after she sets down her bags and sees dinner waiting on the table.

"Can't a girl spend time with her mom?" I ask.

"Sure, but you have done nothing but whine and complain that I have ruined your life by *sentencing* you to community service the rest of the summer. I find it hard to believe you've changed you mind after only one day at the animal shelter."

I shrug my shoulders. "It was a weird day, that's all." The truth is I can't stop thinking about Daisy and all the other animals that are confined to a life living in 3 x 5 foot cages unless a family can be found for them. "Can we get a dog, Mom?" I ask.

"Absolutely not, Evie," Mom says. "I have a hard enough time taking care of you. It's not fair to leave a dog home alone all day without anyone to keep it company."

"But remember how Dad used to tell stories about the dog he owned when he was a little boy? Don't you think if we got a dog that maybe Dad would come home more often?"

34

Mom sighs. "Evie, getting a dog won't bring Dad home." She looks so sad it makes me want to cry, but I'm not ready to hear the truth. Dad needs some time alone. That's all I know and all I want to know.

"Think about it. I'm going to bed. Logan and I want to be at the shelter when it opens tomorrow. Her mom's going to drive us since you go into work later on Tuesdays."

"Good night, Evie. Thanks again for dinner. Be good."

Chapter 6:

The rest of the week has been a blur. It's hard to keep everything that has happened clear in my mind. We have been so busy. Logan's mom has been bringing us to the shelter early every morning and letting us stay later and later. A couple of days we spent eight hours there. I don't love all of our jobs like cleaning out the poop from the kennels or litter boxes or listening to the sounds of thirty dogs all barking to be fed at the same time. But, most of the time Logan and I get to play with the animals. The cats are fun because there's a cat room in the back where we can let out five or six cats at a time. They crawl all over us. Even the kitten who scratched me on the first day is growing on me. When she gets tired out from chasing all the other cats, she likes to curl up on my lap and sleep. Logan and I figured out that Sammy is a girl, so Logan likes to call her

Samantha instead. I think that it's funny that she even cares, since most people think that *Logan* is a boy's name.

"Girls, let's get those dogs walked," says Denise. She still acts tough and important, but she's got a fun side, too. She makes hilarious cartoon character imitations with her voice that crack us up. Even the animals tend to quiet down when high-pitched Mickey Mouse voices come out of her mouth. I tried to copy her voice once when we were outside. Logan laughed so hard that the 60 pound German Shepherd that she'd been walking knocked her to the ground and started licking away the tears of laugher that rolled down her face. It took us ten minutes to settle that dog down.

Logan and I like to do our jobs in a certain order. We like to take the smaller dogs for walks first because they require less energy. Some of the big dogs are real beasts. It takes everything we have to keep them under the control of their leashes. We each have our favorites, too. Logan likes Bo, a huge chocolate Labrador. Denise told her not to get too attached because labs are some of the best family dogs and usually get adopted out fast. It's too late for Logan, though. She puts her whole heart and soul into anything she loves, like that winter break where she spent every day of our vacation skiing on the bunny hill in town until she mastered her new skis. The poor girl should have been covered in bubble wrap by the time she was done. She had a lot of bumps and bruises. Then there was the time when she wanted to impress the new boy in our class who had moved from Mexico. She spent every day after school listening to an old CD on how to speak Spanish that Mom gave her. She even slept with the stupid thing at Marla Kennedy's birthday slumber party. She was so sad when Pedro's dad got a job transfer and moved after a month.

It's no secret to everyone at the shelter that Daisy is the dog that has stolen my heart. I can't walk her, of course. She's still too timid. That doesn't stop me from trying to let her know that she's a pretty special dog, though. When I bring Daisy her food bowl, I always sing *Hush Little Baby, Don't You Cry*. I think that maybe she will be more relaxed if I sing. Dad used to tell me what a nice voice I have.

"Is that Daisy's favorite song?" asks Dr. Mick from behind me.

I jump. "Dr. Mick! You scared me," I say.

"Sorry. I was enjoying your song, that's all."

I smile. "Thanks. Do you think she likes it?"

"Well, it's hard to tell, Evie. She's had a hard life. She scares easily. But the song sounds relaxing, so I bet it helps her."

"Can you tell me about Daisy's life before she came here?" I ask.

Dr. Mick clears his throat. That's something my mom does when she wants to avoid answering me. "That is not an easy question to answer."

"I am not a little kid, Dr. Mick. I'm ten. Plus, maybe I can get Daisy to like me if I understand her life better."

Dr. Mick looks so sad. "Daisy was brought to us a month or so ago. She was in bad shape. The police took her away from a family that hit her, Evie."

"Hit her?" I feel like I've been punched in my own gut. "Why would anyone hit Daisy?"

"We cannot explain why some people act badly. Yes, she was hit and also starved. Neighbors living near Daisy's family finally called the police after seeing Daisy tied up all day and night in all weather conditions with little food and no shelter."

"How did the police know she'd been hit?" I can feel the tears pooling in my eyes.

"Examining Daisy when she first arrived was not easy, Evie. She yelped at everyone near her. But what was odd is that she never showed her teeth. Often when a dog is scared, it will show its teeth, or growl. That was my first clue. I imagine if she showed any aggression, her owners would hit her. Plus, she has a patch under belly that has no hair."

"Why is that?" I ask.

"I don't know for sure. However, I suspect she was hit so hard with something that the hair follicles died. She will forever have that hairless patch of skin."

I don't try to stop the tears anymore. "That's awful. How can we get Daisy to understand that we won't hurt her? That we want to put her with a forever family that will love her and treat her well?"

"Evie, you have a good heart, no matter whether your volunteering here started as your idea or a punishment of your time." He smiles at me. "But we can't save them all, no matter how much we want to. Daisy is going to be sent to a larger shelter near Detroit in a week if she is not adopted. We need to make space for adoptable dogs here."

"But what if she is not adopted there, either?" I ask.

"We are sending Daisy to a new shelter. It has more room. But, Evie, if she is not adopted there, she will likely…um…"

"What, Dr. Mick? She will die? Is that what you are saying?"

"The clinic is a no-kill shelter, but, yes, Daisy will likely spend the rest of her life confined to a kennel in the shelter. Go on, Evie. I am sure there are dogs waiting to be walked."

He leaves me alone at Daisy's cage. I stare at Daisy who is staring at me, waiting for me to leave before she will eat her food. She needs to feel safe, that no one is going to hurt her. I can't let her leave. There has to be a way to save Daisy. There has to be a forever family waiting out there somewhere.

Chapter 7:

I've called a family meeting at Grandma and Grandpa's house tonight. I've even invited my sister Meredith who lives in Grand Rapids. She is too busy with her summer internship to come to the meeting, so I made her promise she'd at least show up with a video chat. Grandpa keeps mumbling about technology destroying the souls of our young people. Grandma calms him down by reminding him that I am serving dinner. Well, I am not exactly serving it, but I am paying for pizza. I used money from my own piggy bank that I have saved from birthday presents and the one month I got paid an allowance. When Meredith complained that she never got paid an allowance for doing chores when she was little, Mom decided that she'd made a good point. No more allowance for me. Meredith is cool most of the time for being a big sister. However, she needs to let go of *the unfairness of her childhood,* as she calls it. That was ten years ago. Ten years is a long time. When she decided to spend the summer in Grand Rapids working to help pay for her college, Mom thought it was a great idea. I cried. No one ever asks me what I want. But tonight, I am leading the family meeting. Someone has to listen to me…for once.

"I'll get it!" I yell as the doorbell rings. The pizza man waits at the door with a large cheese pizza and a small pepperoni pizza. I promised Grandpa I would order pepperoni for him. I pay the pizza man the $18.21 bill. He looks mad when I give him the money. He should be happy that he doesn't have to make change. As I am closing the door with one hand and holding the pizzas with the other, I remember the tip. No wonder the pizza man looked mad. "Wait!" I say. I reach into my pocket and pull out two $1 bills. It's all I have with me. The rest of my money is in my piggy bank across the street. The pizza man smiles, though.

I like making people happy. However, when I shut the door, the pepperoni pizza box slides out from under my arm. I yelp just like Daisy.

Mom and Grandma scrape the pizza off the floor while I put the box with the cheese pizza on the kitchen table. Grandpa stands in the kitchen doorway shaking his head back and forth. Now I've made someone sad.

"It's not that bad," says Mom as she picks up a globby piece of pepperoni pizza from the floor. Almost all of the cheese has slid off the piece and hangs in a glob as she holds it in the air.

"He can't eat that," I say. "It's ruined."

Mom laughs. "He's not eating this piece." She points to the pepperoni box. "There are two pieces that managed to stay in the box."

I sigh. "I'm sorry, Grandpa." This is not how I imagined the beginning of our family meeting. I need everyone to be in a good mood. Pizza gets people in a good mood. I *need* Grandpa to be in a good mood.

At exactly 6:30 p.m., Mom's phone rings. Meredith's face appears when she answers. "Hi, Meredith," says Mom.

Even though Mom supports Meredith spending the summer in Grand Rapids, sometimes I think there's some sort of tension between them. I think Meredith blames Mom for Dad moving away. I don't want to know any more than I have to know. "Hi, Mere," I say as I wave at her from behind Mom's shoulder. "Say *hi* to Grandpa and Grandma." Mom pans the phone for them to wave back. Grandpa has a piece of cheese hanging from his chin. I don't tell him. Sometimes it's better to leave Grandpa alone.

"So, what's the big news, Little Holiday?" asks Meredith. That's my nickname. She's called me Little

Holiday for as long as I can remember. I didn't understand what that name even meant until I turned eight. That's when I connected my name *Evie* to holidays like New Year's *Eve* or Christmas *Eve*. She is the only one that uses that name. I love it.

"I don't have any big news, Mere." My mom and my grandparents settle into the couch and loveseat in my grandparent's living room. I clear my throat. What I have to say is very important. "As most of you know, I have been volunteering my valuable time at the Betsy Willis Animal Shelter."

"That's pretty cool of you, Little Holiday," says Meredith.

I look at my mom who rolls her eyes. "Well, I may not have come up with the idea to volunteer all on my own, *but* I love it now. It's…it's been good for me with Dad gone and all, you know." I know that's not a fair statement.

I'm trying to make my family feel sorry for me. I need all the help I can get. "Anyway, there is a dog at the shelter that needs our help. Her name is Daisy. She's super cute and sweet. The police took her away from her mean family. Those people abused her. Can you believe that?" It makes me want to cry again just thinking about what Dr. Mick told me.

"Evie, stop right now," says Mom. "I told you already that we are not getting a dog. It would be abuse to own a dog that we had to leave home alone for most of the day. You know that. Stop now."

"Mom, I *know* what you said, but if you met Daisy you'd…"

"No, Evie. I will not change my mind," Mom says.

I look at my grandparents and Meredith who is sitting on Grandma's lap, her face looking towards me from the phone. Mr. Stinkypants wraps himself around my ankle,

"Anyway, Daisy is going to a larger shelter near Detroit next week if she can't find a home here. Denise says that if she's not adopted there, she will die there, not right away, of course, but eventually she will live out her life on a cold cement floor in a cage. What kind of a life is that for such a good dog?"

"What's wrong with her?" asks Grandpa. He has never been one for hiding his thoughts.

"Nothing is wrong with her, Grandpa," I say.

"Little Holiday, what's the *rest* of the story?" Meredith asks.

"Well..." I hesitate too long. Mom stands up. She starts walking toward the kitchen. "Wait! Okay, fine, I'll tell you. She's a big baby. Everything scares her to death. She won't eat her food until she knows no one is watching her. She won't look anyone in the eye. She hides her tail between her legs. She cries like a baby if anyone gets close."

Now I am crying, and it's not to get someone to feel sorry for me. I only feel sorry for Daisy.

"Evie," Grandma grabs my hand. "Grandpa and I love animals. You know that." She pets Mr. Stinkypants as if to prove her point. "Remember the toad you rescued in the window well last spring? Who took care of it for you when your mom wouldn't let you keep it in the house?"

"You did, Grandma," I say.

"Yes, and who let you feed that stray cat that kept visiting the neighborhood even when it pooped in your Grandpa's prize roses and drove Mr. Stinkypants crazy at the window?"

I try not to smile. "You did, Grandma."

"Yes, but we can't take Daisy. She needs a lot of love. We have that to give, but we are not at the point in our lives to nurse a damaged dog. We don't know how to do it."

"She's not damaged," I say. "She's perfectly healthy. Dr. Mick told me so himself."

"She is damaged." Grandma puts her hand on her chest. "Right here, in the heart. Her spirit is broken. I don't know how you can fix that," she says.

"You can't fix the world, Little Holiday. The world doesn't work like that," says Meredith.

"I thought my family was more caring than this. Is that why Dad left...because you didn't love him enough?" I know I shouldn't have said those things. I didn't really mean them. I miss Dad. I am sad for Daisy. I run out of my grandparent's house and cross the street. When I get to my house, I scribble a note that I am going to Logan's house. Then I crumple it up and throw it away. Why should I tell my family where I am going? Then I sprint down the street away from my family, away from the only people I thought I could count on to do what's right.

Chapter 8:

Mom let me spend the night at Logan's house. She showed up after dinner to talk to Logan's parents. I guess she found my note in the trash. She told me before she left that I was grounded, starting the next day. After I got home from the shelter, I was to check in with my grandparents. Then I was to clean my room and vacuum the living room. And if I even thought of turning on the television, there would be more trouble for me. She took my iPod away, too.

I know Logan's parents would adopt Daisy if they could, but Logan's little brother has asthma. It's so bad that Logan has to throw her clothes in the washing machine as soon as she gets home from the animal shelter so that the dog and cat germs don't spread around the house. Sometimes I wish Logan's brother and I could switch families. That might solve all my problems.

Janet waves at Logan and me when we get to the shelter. She tosses us each a wrapped piece of hard candy as we head toward the back. I put the candy in my pocket for a snack. A family is petting one of the former fighting dogs outside of its pen. The dog's name is Rocco. He almost pulls my arm off when I try to control him during walks, but he doesn't have a mean bone in his body. He just loves to get where he's supposed to be. Maybe today that place will be in the home of this friendly-looking family. I hope so.

"Let's clean the cat room first. I want to say *goodbye* to Samantha," says Logan.

"Goodbye?"

"Yes. Evie, don't be a dunce. You know this is the last day we have to volunteer."

"I am not a dunce! I know it's the last day we *had* to volunteer, but I thought we would keep coming for the rest of the summer. We love it here, Logan!"

"I know we do, but Mom signed me up for soccer camp next week. Then we have our family vacation in July."

I sit down on the floor of the cat room. Logan opens cages to let the better-behaved cats mix with each other. An orange and white striped cat rolls a ball of yarn across the floor. "I can't come if your mom doesn't drive me. My mom works in the opposite direction of the shelter. Plus, her hours wouldn't make it easy for her to bring me. Stupid job." I pick up a gray kitten and bury my face in its fur so Logan doesn't know that I am about to cry.

"I'm sorry, Evie. I am. We've had a lot of fun here and done some great things for the dogs and cats. It almost makes getting into trouble worth it. This was the best punishment we've ever had. Maybe *Evie and the Volunteers* needs to find another way to save the world."

"Maybe," I say. "But it won't be the same."

I am putting food into dog bowls when Denise walks up behind me. "Hi, Evie."

"Hi," I say.

"I sure am going to miss you guys around here. I can honestly say I've never had a crazier group of volunteers. You kept me on my toes, but you have a heart of gold. The animals were very lucky to have known you."

"Thanks, Denise." I give her a big bear hug. I think it surprises her because she almost falls over. Only the wall behind her stops her from falling.

"Well, anyway, I've got to help Janet with some adoption paperwork. You go on and feed the dogs. You know they don't like to wait."

I nod my head and wait for her to leave the room before I fill one bowl with a little extra food. I take Daisy's bowl to her cage. Something different hangs on the bars of the kennel. I pull the paper from the clip that holds it in place.

Prepare for transfer.

I look around the cages and see only one other cage with such a note. This cage belongs to a large white dog that never gets walked without a muzzle and only by an adult, usually Dr. Mick who is strong enough to control her. These are the dogs going to Detroit. These are the dogs no one wants. My heart breaks into a thousand more pieces.

Daisy is sleeping with one eye open in the back corner of the cage, her safe place. When I set down her bowl of food, she open both eyes and jerks her head upright. I sing *Hush Little Baby, Don't You Cry*. When I am

57

on my third round of the song, which is one round more than usual and I'm having to make up words, something happens that makes my heart happy again.

Daisy stands up. It is like a showdown in the Wild West. She stands in one corner of the cage. I stand outside the bars on the opposite corner. She takes one step toward her bowl. I keep singing in a soft voice. She takes another step. And then another. And then another. I keep singing until she is standing mere inches from me on the other side of the cage in front of her bowl. She stares at me. I stop singing. Then she puts her head in the food bowl and eats every last bit of food, even the extra I gave this time.

I want to pet her through the bars, but I know that is not what I should do. Instead, I talk. "I am so sorry I couldn't find you a forever family, Daisy. You will always be in my heart. That might not help you much, but it helps me to know that you trust me now. I know there is a great family dog inside of you. Someone just needs to take that chance."

"She knows you care, Evie." It's Dr. Mick again. He is good at surprising me. "That's the greatest gift you can give another living creature—to let them feel loved."

I start to think of my family and how mean I was to them last night. "Thanks, Dr. Mick. Thanks for everything. I'm really going to miss you."

"I'll miss you and Logan, too, Evie. Come back and visit us anytime."

"Uh, Logan's Mom is going to be here soon. Do you mind if I say *goodbye* in private—I mean—to Daisy?"

"Take your time. I have appointments back at the clinic."

When Dr. Mick has left, I feel like it's just Daisy and me even though all the dogs are barking again since Dr. Mick closed the door. Daisy has finished her food but moved back to her safe spot in the kennel. I look around to make sure that no one is listening. I don't want anyone to think I am as crazy as I feel talking to a dog like she can understand me. I hope she can understand me. "Thank you for reminding me how important it is to treat other living things, Daisy. Sorry you haven't been as lucky as me to find a loving family. I hope the new shelter has great people to love you like the people here do. I'm going home to let my family know how much I appreciate them and how sorry I am for being a big baby because I didn't get my way." I blow Daisy a kiss and walk away from her cage. I don't look back because I know that if I do, I might never leave.

Chapter 9:

I ask Logan's Mom to stop at the wildflower stand along one of the country roads we pass on our way from the shelter to my home. I use some of my birthday money to buy two bouquets of flowers—one for Grandma and one for Mom. It's a start.

Grandma and Grandpa have Bunco night at the senior center this evening. I'm not sure why throwing dice is so exciting to them, but they love it. Grandpa likes anything where there is a chance to win money. Mom is working late, but she told Grandma to let me come home when they leave for game night. I will actually be home an entire hour by myself. After promising my grandparents that all the doors are locked, that I won't turn on the oven, that I won't answer the door, and all of the other million things I have to promise to, they leave. I take the leftover chicken and rice casserole from their dinner and put it in the refrigerator for Mom to heat up later.

I can't watch television because I am still grounded, though I do consider it, because how would Mom know? I remember that this is my night for saying *I'm sorry*, and breaking a rule, whether known or unknown to the rule-maker, would not be a good idea.

I put the wildflowers in a vase on the middle of the kitchen table. When I hear the garage door coming up, I know that Mom is home. She will be surprised to find that I've heated her plate of dinner again. But it is me that is surprised to see that she is not alone.

"Hi, Evie," says Dad. He gives a slight wave in my direction.

I wave back. "Hi, Dad," I whisper because that's all the air that comes out of my mouth. It's been months since I've seen my dad. We only talk on the phone once a week, and that call lasts about five minutes before we have run out of things to say. I feel like I might be sick.

Mom takes over. "Evie, did you put those flowers out?" She doesn't wait for an answer. "They're lovely. I see you have dinner ready, too. How thoughtful. Dad and I grabbed a bite to eat after I picked him up from the train station. Maybe you could put the food in a container, and I'll take it to work for lunch tomorrow? I sure do love your Grandma's chicken and rice casserole."

Mom is spending too much time talking about unimportant things. The real question is *why is Dad here after all these months?* Of course I got used to him being gone in the war across the ocean. He had three different tours he got called over for. Each time he was gone almost a year. But when he came back for good six months ago, things were different. Dad didn't talk a lot. He didn't go back to work building houses with Uncle Don. He didn't really do much of anything. Then, just like that, he was gone again. Mom said he needed some quiet time alone, but I don't know what he was doing. Meredith and Mom didn't talk about it. And everyone treated me like things were normal, even Grandma and Grandpa. "What's going on, Mom?" I ask.

Mom sighs. "Evie, your dad and I have some more things to talk about, but everything's going to be fine. You'll see."

"I don't understand," I say.

"We will talk again in the morning. Say *good night* to your Dad."

I look at my dad. He is sitting at the table, his eyes darting around the kitchen, like he's waiting for something to move. When I touch his arm, he flinches. His skin is cold. "*Good night,* Dad."

At the sound of his name, his muscles soften. Even the hard lines in his face relax. "Sorry, Evie. I bet this is confusing. It's really nice to see you."

"I'll...I'll see you in the morning, I guess?"

"I'll be here," he says. He must sense my doubt because he adds, "I promise."

Chapter 10:

The house is quiet when I wake up. It's not until after my shower that I remember I am not alone after all. Mom is gone to work, like usual, but Dad is still here. I don't know why I expected him to go with her to work. It just seems strange that he will be here in the house all day while we are gone. At least, I think I'll be gone. I don't know if I am supposed to stay home with Dad or go to my grandparent's house. I really wish I was going to the shelter today. Why did Logan have to leave for soccer camp? One thought leads to another which gives me the best idea I've had in a long time.

"Dad?"

He pauses the television. He is watching some old show from the 1990s on one of those channels that my mom likes to watch when she's alone—something about walking down memory lane. "Good morning, Evie."

"Uh, I was wondering if you could give me a ride somewhere—it's somewhere Mom approves, so you don't need to worry about that."

"I would love to go for a drive. I haven't driven in months. I guess we'll have to take the motorcycle, though, since Mom has the car. Do you think your helmet still fits?"

He's being so parent-like, I'm a bit off-center. Then I remember the motorcycle and my little accident at the beginning of summer break. "Dad, I had a little accident with your motorcycle."

He stands up and raises his voice. It startles me. "You took the motorcycle out?"

"No, no—nothing like that. I just knocked it over."

Dad takes a very slow, deep breath and sits down. "Oh, okay, that's fine. You scared me half to death, Evie. Don't scare your dad like that."

"Sorry. I really am sorry about knocking it over, too."

"It was an accident."

"Uh, more like a careless incident, but actually that is kind of why I need a ride."

I explain my community service punishment for sneaking out of my grandparent's house, knocking over his motorcycle, and losing my bike at the beach. Then, after Dad examines the motorcycle to discover a few new scratches and a minor dent, but nothing worse, and I find my helmet which I have to squeeze my head in to, we start our trip to the Besty Willis Animal Shelter.

Even though I've traveled the same route to the shelter for the last two weeks, there's something different about riding there on the back of a motorcycle. Every sense seems more alive. I inhale the dry, humid summer air and listen to the birds chirping in the trees that overhang some of the roads. Dad drives a lot more slowly than I remember, but maybe he's enjoying the view as much as me. I squeeze him a little tighter because it's nice to have him home.

"Evie, it sure didn't take very long for you to come back!" Everyone should start their day with a smile from Janet.

"Janet, this is my Dad. Is it okay if I show him around?"

Janet looks at Dad and gives him her friendly grin. "Of course, it is. But Denise might put you to work!"

"That's fine with me."

Denise does exactly what Janet warned. She puts me to work. Secretly, though, I don't mind at all. Even Dad gets in on the fun scooping litter boxes. He's smiled more in the half hour we've been here than he did all last night.

"How many cats get adopted every month?" he asks as a black and white cat crawls up his shirt.

"Denise says that about 20 cats are adopted every month, but they take in at least 30."

"So, there's never enough homes, I guess."

"No. It makes me sad," I say.

"It makes me sad, too," says Dad. He sets the cat back in its cage and ruffles my hair. I'm sure glad to have Dad back.

"Let's go see the dogs. They're a lot of fun, too," I say. I grab Dad's hand, which is something I haven't done since I was a little girl, and pull him toward the dog kennels.

Dad covers his ears when we enter the kennel commons. I'm used to the sound, but I know he isn't. His face is pale.

"Are you okay, Dad?" I ask. "They'll settle down in a little bit. They think they're all getting food or going for a walk." I smile, but he doesn't. I squeeze his hand a little tighter. He follows me slowly. I show him the dogs and give him some of their histories. "That poodle was found living under someone's porch. It got sprayed by a skunk. You should have smelled him when he got here, even though he'd already been given five baths! Phew! It was pretty strong. This special blueberry bath Denise knows about finally did the trick." Dad softens his grip on my hand. "And this is Mona. She's part Basset Hound." On cue, Mona howls. "Isn't that the funniest sound ever?" There are three families that want Mona. The shelter is picking her best forever family."

"Forever family?" asks Dad, as the dogs start to quiet down.

"Yes, every dog has a family that it belongs with, but sometimes it takes some bad times in life before the dog finds that perfect family. It's sad, but the shelter tries to make the dogs and cats *and* the families happy. They say they like to complete the perfect family. Isn't that cool?"

Dad nods his head. "Forever family," Dad repeats.

"Oh, no!" I scream when we get to the final kennel in the room.

Dad drops to his knees and faces me, grabbing me by the shoulders. "Evie, what's the matter?"

My tears answer first. Something is very wrong. Then I point to the empty cage. "She's gone," I say.

"Who's gone?" asks Dad.

"Daisy," I say.

"Who's Daisy?" asks Dad.

"Daisy is…Daisy is…she's…"

Denise comes to my rescue. "Hello, I'm Denise. I'm the assistant director here." She shakes Dad's hand. He stands up. "What Evie is trying to say is that Daisy is a special dog with a sad story. She's not easily adoptable, though, so we are moving her to another shelter in Detroit tomorrow. She's been moved to a kennel in the back. We are waiting on the truck to get here for her."

"She's not gone yet?" I ask, wiping away my tears.

"No, you can go see her, Evie."

I run through the kennel commons to the door that leads to the back of the shelter, the all-purpose storage room which also has a garage door. Maybe they don't want the other dogs to get sad seeing Daisy leave. Denise reads my thoughts. "Daisy might not load easily, so we moved her away from the other animals so there won't be a scene." Daisy looks so sad sitting in her cage. It really is a cage, too, about half the size of her normal kennel. Poor girl. "I will give the three of you some alone time. Let me know if you need anything," says Denise.

Dad is standing behind me. He is very quiet. I feel a little crazy, but one look at Daisy and my heart breaks. She needs to know someone that loves her is here, so I sing. As I do, Daisy lifts her head. She lets out a sigh and rests her chin on her front paws. If a dog has stress, I think she let some of it go.

"Tell me about Daisy's life," says Dad. He is sitting on the floor next to me.

"Some people abused her. I can't even call them her family because real families should not treat each other the way Daisy was treated. They hit her and starved her. Can you believe that, Dad? They left her outside all the time no matter what the weather was like, and they did not give her shelter to protect her. Now she can't stand to be touched by anyone. She hides in the corner and cries if people get too close. She's so sweet, Dad, but people are afraid to take a chance on letting her into their homes. She might not know how to be loved." When I am done talking, I turn to Dad. He is crying, not the loud, ugly kind of cry, but little tears are spilling out of his eyes. I have never seen my dad cry before. "Dad, what's wrong?" I ask.

He clears his throat and wipes his tears away, like he's embarrassed to have been caught crying. "Evie, you know I love you, right?"

"Of course I do, Dad," I say.

"I will be home soon," says Dad. "I promise."

"What do you mean, Dad?" I ask. "You're home now."

"I am, Evie. But I still have some more work to do."

"I don't understand."

"I know you don't, but things are getting better. I feel a lot better. And your story about Daisy has helped me to see that." I wait for him to explain what he means. "You and your mom and your sister, even though she's grown up now, are my forever family."

"I know that, Dad."

"Sometimes it takes a little time to figure things out when you've been through…a lot."

I think Dad's talking about the war, but I'm not sure. "Everything's going to be okay, Dad." I wrap my arms around him.

"It is, Evie." Dad smiles bigger than I have ever seen him smile before. "And I think I might be able to help with the Daisy problem."

"What do you mean?" I say because now I'm getting excited.

"I have to go back to Detroit, for a few more months. I'm getting good help there, Evie. Trust me. I am doing everything I can to get the help I need to make our forever family even stronger. But, it's lonely, and I think that maybe Daisy and I would be good for each other. And then, when I am ready to come back home full time, maybe

Daisy will trust us a little more, and maybe we could be one, big happy family and—,"

"Dad! Really? But, what about Mom?"

"Yeah, that might be a problem, but I think if she sees how good this could be for me and you and Daisy, then maybe we can convince her."

"Let's fill out the papers, Dad! We don't have a lot of time!" I look at Daisy resting in her cage. I whisper to her. "Daisy, we'll be back. This time you're coming with us...Uh, Dad, how do you carry a dog on a motorcycle?"

He starts laughing, and so do I.

Chapter 11:

We have to wait for Mom to get home to pick up Daisy. Dad had a hush-hush phone call with her from their bedroom. It went on for a long time, but when Dad came out of the bedroom he gave me the thumbs-up sign. Daisy is coming home, not this home yet, but soon. When Dad is better, she will come home to *this home*, our family's home. I feel a whole lot of mixed-up emotions right now. I am excited that we saved Daisy. I am sad that Dad is leaving again tomorrow. Right now, though, Dad is giving orders like he's back in the army.

"Clear out the downstairs bathroom. Take out the toilet paper roll. Empty the trash. Better yet, just take the trash can out of the bathroom—less things for her to stick her nose in. Find a couple of old blankets—soft ones. Set up a nice bed for Daisy. When I get back to Detroit I'll get her a proper blanket. And then we need to…"

"Dad, slow down. I can't do everything at the same time."

"Sorry, Evie. I—it's hard to explain. I want Daisy to feel safe, to know we will protect her."

"I want that, too, Dad." He hugs me tight. "I think it's time you tell me why you really left home, Daddy. I haven't called him *Daddy* in a very long time. "I'm old enough to know."

Dad sighs. "I suppose you are. Sit down, Evie." I sit at the kitchen table across from him. "Tell me what you know," he says.

"I know that when you came home from the war you said you'd never go back there again, that your time was done. But, then you left again anyway." Dad looks so sad, but I have to tell him the truth.

"But I didn't go back to the war, Evie."

"You still left. What's the difference to me?"

Dad covers his face with his hands and rubs his forehead. It is quiet for a while. "I suppose to you there was no difference, and in a way I am glad that there was no difference. You don't need to be worried about your dad."

"But I do worry. I just don't know what I'm worrying about."

"Evie, war is hard. I did things...I saw things...I have memories that I can't erase from my mind."

I shake my head like I understand. I don't really, but I can imagine. I have watched the news. I have seen pictures of what it is like in the Middle East even though I'm not exactly sure where that place even is. "Were you scared in the war, Daddy?"

Dad looks past me like he's not even here sitting in our kitchen. Then he shakes his head and he's back. "Sometimes I was scared, Evie."

"You know what Daisy's feeling then, huh?" I ask.

"I know what it's like to be uncertain about what's going to happen next. I've been around a lot of hurt."

"Daisy's lucky, Dad," I say.

"Why's that?" he asks.

"Because you are going to do everything you can to let her know she's safe and won't ever hurt her," I say.

"Yes, that's exactly what I'm going to do. But I'm not going to do it alone." He hugs me again. "Evie, the doctors say I have something called PTSD. It stands for Post-Traumatic Stress Syndrome."

"Are you sick, Daddy?"

"No, no. It's not like that. I am just having a hard time being back from the war because it's hard to forget some of the things that happened. I am getting help from a treatment center that was created to help war veterans to get used to feeling safe again and not focus so much on what they lived through in the war. I already feel so much

81

better. Knowing that I'm not crazy—I mean, that I'm not alone in my feelings—makes me feel better. I'll be home for good very soon. Do you have any questions?"

"I'm glad you told me. I understand now."

"Good. Let's get back to work. Mom will be here in an hour to pick us up to get Daisy."

Mom doesn't talk a lot on the way to the Betsy Willis Animal Shelter. She looks a little bit mad but not so mad like she is going to yell at anyone. I don't think she is convinced that bringing Daisy home, even for one night before Dad leaves, is a good idea.

The shelter is about to close for the day. Janet and Denise and Dr. Mick are all waiting for us in the back with Daisy. Dr. Mick greets us first. "Hello, Mr. and Mrs. Quin. I'm Dr. Mick. So glad to meet the parents of this charming *and* convincing young one." He points at me. I smile.

"Nice to meet you, Dr. Mick," says Mom. "but I can assure you that Evie was not the convincing one. This decision comes from my husband."

"With my wife's support," my dad quickly adds.

"Yes. Mr. Quin, with your permission, I spoke with the director of the PTSD clinic in Detroit. I want to make sure that the best interests of you *and* Daisy are met."

Dad looks like he is holding his breath. I understand, though. All families that want to adopt a shelter animal have to get proper screening. Even though they know me, they don't know my family.

"The director has confidence that Daisy will be a good addition to your family. Although Daisy is not a trained therapy dog, he believes that pets provide positive support to PTSD patients. I have to be honest, Mr. Quin. I am both excited and nervous about Daisy's adoption. I am thrilled that she is getting a loving home. However, I don't know yet whether Daisy will ever be able to accept love from a family because of what she has been through in life. But if anyone should try, it should be Evie's family." Dr. Mick smiles at me. "And I have contacted the Detroit animal shelter where Daisy was headed. They will welcome her if...if things don't work out."

"We will do our very best to make things work out," says Dad.

Daisy starts yelping when Denise opens the cage. There's nothing we can do to prepare her for what's to come. If only she understood how much better things are going to be. Denise puts a gentle leader collar around Daisy's neck and pulls her carefully toward the front of the kennel. Daisy cries louder. It makes me want to cry, too. I start singing our song. I feel foolish, but I don't care. Making Daisy feel safe is more important. By the time I get to the third round of *Hush Little Baby, Don't You Cry*, Daisy is just whimpering. Dad and Dr. Mick have to kind of push Daisy along because she does *not* want to use her legs to walk to the car, but at least she doesn't completely stop.

Before we leave, Janet hands us the adoption packet that all adoptive families get when a new pet goes home. I hug her *goodbye* again. I look at Daisy lying on my soft princess blanket in the backseat. She is panting hard and still making whimpering sounds that cross over into howling sounds. I get to sit by her on the trip home. And I could not be happier.

Chapter 12:

I slept with Daisy in the bathroom last night. Mom did not agree with the plan, but Dad said I could. Mom did not argue with him. I am going to miss him when he leaves today. I can't believe Daisy only got to stay at our house for one night, but I know that when she comes back the next time, it will be forever. Plus, Dad will stay, too. Meredith called this morning. She is going to help Dad get Daisy settled in his apartment. She told me on the phone that Dad's apartment is close to where he is getting his treatment for the PTSD. She told me that she was kind of mad when he left but that she understands better now. I think PTSD is confusing for the whole family.

Daisy has stopped crying, but she won't leave the bathroom floor. I think she really likes my princess blanket. It's been my favorite blanket since I was a little girl, but Daisy needs it more than me.

The doorbell rings. Mom yells my name. Logan is standing in the living room. "Hi! Did you come to see Daisy before she leaves" I ask.

"You know I did! Plus, I have some more great news. I have another idea for *Evie and the Volunteers*," she says.

"What do you mean?" I ask.

"When I get back from vacation in a week, Mom said she wants me to stay busy. My Great-Aunt Joey went into Woodland Nursing Home a couple of weeks ago. It's that old nursing home on the right side of the road if you're leaving town on the highway. Anyway, when she last visited they were advertising for student volunteers to help the old people."

"What would we do?"

"I'm not sure…maybe play bingo or take the people in wheelchairs for rides."

I sit down on the couch. I was really hoping that Mom would find a way to reward me for saving Dad and Daisy. Well, maybe that's a stretch, but I did do something good, and thinking of helping other people takes a lot of work.

"I think extending your community service is a great idea," Mom says laughing. Dad is standing behind her and puts his hand on her shoulder and squeezes.

"You all find this pretty funny, don't you?" I say. "I was kind of thinking we might do something fun like take a trip or buy a swimming pass for the pool, or…"

"I think volunteering at the nursing home *will* be fun, Evie. Come on!" says Logan.

Daisy lets out a bark, a real bark, not a whiny howl. We all turn to see her standing in the hallway next to the living room. "Daisy, you came out of the bathroom!" I say.

"I think Daisy wants you to keep volunteering," says Logan.

Daisy barks again. My family laughs as she continues to bark. Every time we laugh, she barks again. It's like a game. I see a hint of joy in Daisy's eyes that I have never seen before. "Fine, Daisy. I'll go the nursing home. But don't get any ideas! I'm not adopting a grandpa! I've already got one of those! And that's enough!"

Maybe this summer isn't going to be so bad after all.

Evie and the Volunteers Series

Join ten-year-old Evie and her friends as they volunteer all over town meeting lots of cool people and getting into just a little bit of trouble. There is no place left untouched by their presence, and what they get from the people they meet is greater than any amount of money.

Book 1 *Animal Shelter*

Book 2 *Nursing Home*

Book 3 *Coming September 2016*

Book 4 *Coming Winter 2016*

Check out the first chapter of Book 2, *Evie and the Volunteers, Nursing Home*

Chapter 1:

Dad and Daisy have been video chatting with Mom and me almost every night before bed. Well, really Dad talks to us while Daisy sits on my princess blanket on the floor behind him in the corner of the bathroom. One might think it is strange to talk to her dad every night in the bathroom, but since that is the only place where Daisy is comfortable, it's fine by me. Dad says that Daisy usually only comes out of the bathroom when she has to go outside to use her own bathroom, but she doesn't yelp anymore. That's a good thing since Dad is living in an apartment building until he feels ready to come home. Dad's still getting help for his post-traumatic stress disorder, or PTSD, after being a soldier in the war for a long time. The doctors are helping him learn to deal with some tough things he experienced in the war. Daisy had a rough life once, too. Now Dad and Daisy are helping each other. I'm glad that Daisy doesn't cry every night like she used to do. I don't think his neighbors would like to hear Daisy crying all night long. Dad says that even though Daisy doesn't want to go on walks or play catch or anything like that, it's nice having her there for company. He says that she is relaxing. I can see that Dad is relaxing, too. He smiles a lot more than he used to.

"Evie, Logan's mom is here!" yells Mom from the living room.

I grab my lunch bag from the kitchen—ham sandwich (no mayo), an apple, and a bag of chips—and head to the front door. "See you after work," I say.

"Wait! Come back here," says Mom. She puts her hands on my shoulders, bends down a little, and looks me straight in the eye. This must be serious. "Old people are not dogs and cats."

I roll my eyes. "Duh, Mom," I say.

"I'm serious, Evie. You need to be respectful. Not everyone is going to be in a good mood. Not everyone is going to feel well. Be kind even if it's hard."

"Mom, I'm used to dealing with Grandpa when he's crabby. It's no big deal. I've got this!" I give her a quick hug goodbye and walk out the door. She worries way too much.

Logan is talking a mile a minute before I even get my seatbelt on. "I can't wait for you to meet my Great-Aunt Joey—well, I just call her Aunt Joey, but she's really my Grandma Cara's sister. You remember Grandma Cara, right? She's the one that moved to that awesome retirement community in Florida after Grandpa Rudy died. So, anyway, Aunt Joey lived alone, but she's a little clumsy. She kept falling. The last time she fell, she ended up breaking a bone in her leg, so her kids, my Aunt Vicky and Uncle Wally, decided she should stay at Woodland Nursing Home until she gets better. She is going to be so happy to see me, isn't she, Mom?" Mrs. Nelson shakes her head *yes*. My head is spinning from all the talking going on from the front seat.

"Yes, Logan," says Mrs. Nelson. "Aunt Joey is going to be thrilled to see you. You are her spitting image."

"That's what my family always says," says Logan. I think she is blushing. "Did I tell you, Evie, that Aunt Joey was a famous Hollywood actress before she moved back to Michigan to raise her family? They called her *Josephine Nelson*. She knew Harrison Ford—you know the guy that played Indiana Jones and Han Solo? Isn't that cool? My family says I should try out for the fall musical at school. You know, it's in my genes." She laughs.

It's my turn to talk. "Logan, your aunt sounds awesome. But can you calm down a little? I mean, I don't think all the people at Woodland Nursing Home have such exciting pasts."

"How do you know that, Evie? I think everyone lives an exciting life. You just have to take the time to find out," says Logan.

Mrs. Nelson turns into the parking lot of Woodland Nursing Home. The two-story building looks welcoming with three large pots of red geraniums sitting out front. An older man is sitting in a wheelchair by the front door. When we get out of the car and walk by him on our way into the building, he smiles and waves. He doesn't have a lot of hair, and what he does have is blowing over the top of his head. He looks like a gray-haired peacock. Something in his lap blows away, floating in the air before it drops to the ground next to the pot of geraniums.

"Uh-oh," says the old man.

His eyes meet mine, and I understand without a word spoken aloud that whatever blew away was pretty important. I bend down to pick up a picture. It is old. The corners of the picture are bent, and the black and white photo seems faded from being held so much. A man and woman are holding hands, looking into each other's eyes. The same smile on the man in the picture matches the smile the old man gave before the wind took his picture for a ride.

Logan and her mom are already in the building. They walked right past the man. I return the picture to him. His smile gets even bigger.

"Thank you. Thank you," he says. "She doesn't like to fly."

I don't understand what he is talking about. I have heard that some people in nursing homes don't have things all clear in their minds anymore.

He laughs. "Libby didn't like to fly in airplanes," he says. "I was trying to make a joke about the picture flying out of my hands and my wife not liking to fly." He raises one corner of his mouth in a playful way that kind of reminds me of…well, myself. Mom says that's how she can tell when I'm about to be up to no good. I like this guy already.

"I like your joke," I say. I wave *hello* with my hand in the air.

"My name is *Royce*, but people around here call me RJ because there's a Royce down in Wing B of the building, and I'm the young, good-looking Royce." I must look confused because he explains. "*Royce Joseph, RJ*. Get it?" He laughs again. RJ is funny.

"My name is *Evie*. I have to go now, RJ, but maybe I'll be seeing you around. My friend Logan and I are volunteering for the next few weeks."

RJ nods his head slowly before he speaks. "My wife's a real beauty."

He's still staring at the picture when I leave him to run inside to find Logan and her mom.

Other Children's Books by Marcy Blesy:

Confessions of a Corn Kid:

Twelve-year-old Bernie Taylor doesn't fit in. She wants to be an actress but not your typical country-music lovin', beef-eatin' actress you'd expect from Cornville, Illinois. No way. She wants to go to Chicago to be a real actress, just like her mom did before she died of breast cancer. Bernie keeps a journal that her Mom gave her and writes down all her confessions, the deepest feelings of her heart, 'cause she doesn't want any of those regrets Mom talked about. Regrets sound too much like those bubbly blisters she keeps getting on her feet from trying to fit into last year's designer knock-off shoes. But it's not easy for Bernie to pursue her dreams. Her dad just doesn't understand. Plus, she's tired of being bullied for being different. Why can't middle schoolers wear runway fashions?

Then, during the announcement of the sixth grade play, Bernie's teacher reveals that there will be one scholarship to a prestigious performing arts camp in Chicago. Bernie knows it's her one big chance to achieve her dream. She spends too much time dreaming of the lead role in the play (which includes kissing Cameron Edmunds) and not enough time practicing her audition lines. She bumbles her lines, blows her audition, and battles her bully, Dixie Moxley, reigning Jr. Miss Corn Harvest Queen. She digs in with the heels of her hand-me-down knee-high boots, determined to win that scholarship-somehow. If she doesn't, she'll be stuck in Cornville forever, far away from the spotlight she craves.

Am I Like My Daddy?

Join seven-year-old Grace on her journey through coping with the loss of her father while learning about the different ways that people grieve the loss of a loved one. In the process of learning about who her father was through the eyes of others, she learns about who she is today because of her father's personality and love. *Am I Like My Daddy?* is a book designed to help children who are coping with the loss of a loved one. Children are encouraged to express through journaling what may be so difficult to express through everyday conversation. *AILMD* teaches about loss through reflection.

Am I Like My Daddy? is an important book in the children's grief genre. Many books in this genre deal with the time immediately after a loved one dies. This book focuses on years after the death, when a maturing child is reprocessing his or her grief. New questions arise in the child's need to fill in those memory gaps.

Be the Vet:

Do you like dogs and cats?

Have you ever thought about being a veterinarian?

Place yourself as the narrator in seven unique stories about dogs and cats. When a medical emergency or illness impacts the pet, you will have the opportunity to diagnose the problem and suggest treatment. Following each story is the treatment plan offered by Dr. Ed Blesy, a 16 year practicing veterinarian. You will learn veterinary terms and diagnoses while being entertained with fun, interesting stories.

This is the first book in the BE THE VET series.

For ages 9-12

I would like to thank my beta readers—Connor, Luke, Anne, Summer, and Clara—for all of their insightful comments. Young minds are great teachers. Thank you to my family and friends for their continued support. And thank you to my students for providing the joy and frustration that inspire my writing—never a dull moment.

Made in the USA
Coppell, TX
22 June 2020